SWISS FAMILY ROBINSON

SWISS FAMILY ROBINSON

BY JOHANN WYSS
ADAPTED BY DAISY ALBERTO
ILLUSTRATED BY ROBERT HUNT

A STEPPING STONE BOOK™
Random House New York

To my own bold Jack
—D.A.

For Lynn
—R.H.

Text copyright © 2006 by Daisy Alberto. Illustrations copyright © 2006 by Robert Hunt. All rights reserved. Published in the United States by Random House Children's Books, a division of Random House, Inc., New York.

www.steppingstonesbooks.com
www.randomhouse.com/kids

Educators and librarians, for a variety of teaching tools, visit us at www.randomhouse.com/teachers

Library of Congress Cataloging-in-Publication Data
Alberto, Daisy.
Swiss family Robinson / by Johann Wyss ; adapted by Daisy Alberto ; illustrated by Robert Hunt. — 1st ed.
    p.   cm.
"A Stepping Stone Book."
SUMMARY: Relates the fortunes of a shipwrecked family as they imaginatively adapt to life on an island with abundant animal and plant life.
ISBN-13: 978-0-375-87525-0 (pbk.) — ISBN-13: 978-0-375-97525-7 (lib. bdg.)
ISBN-10: 0-375-87525-5 (pbk.) — ISBN-10: 0-375-97525-X (lib. bdg.)
[1. Survival—Fiction. 2. Family life—Fiction. 3. Islands—Fiction.]
I. Hunt, Robert, ill. II. Wyss, Johann David, 1743–1818. Schweizerische Robinson. III. Title.
PZ7.A3217Swi 2006   [Fic]—dc22   2006001099

Printed in the United States of America   10 9 8 7 6 5
First Edition

CONTENTS

1

Shipwrecked and Alone

For many days our ship had been tossed at sea. The storm raged and raged. Above us, the seamen yelled frantically to each other.

My heart sank as I looked around the cabin at my family. My brave wife was trying to calm the children. Our four sons were filled with terror.

Suddenly I heard a cry. At the same time, the ship struck something! Water poured in on all sides.

"Lower the boats!" the captain shouted.

I rushed on deck. The last lifeboat was already pushing off! I begged the sailors to wait for us. But it was too late.

After a moment, however, I saw that our position wasn't as bad as I had thought. The stern, or back of the ship, was jammed between two rocks. The rocks kept the ship from sinking. And through the rain, I could see land!

I returned to my family. "Courage, dear ones!" I said. "Our ship is secure and there is land nearby. We should be able to go ashore tomorrow!"

By morning, the storm had passed. I woke the boys. My wife and our youngest son, Franz, fed the animals on board. The rest of us gathered supplies we would need onshore.

We found guns, bullets, tools, and fish-hooks. My wife told us there were also some chickens, ducks, geese, and pigeons, and a cow, a donkey, two goats, six sheep, a ram, and a pig on board. And Jack had discovered two friendly dogs!

"Excellent," I said. "But how will we get everything to shore?"

"Why can't we each get into a tub and float there?" asked Jack. "That's what I do on our pond at home."

"Capital idea!" I cried.

We sawed four large barrels in half. I nailed them together into a makeshift boat and added poles to give it balance. The boys brought oars.

We stowed everything that we would need in the tubs. Then we set the ship's ducks, geese, and pigeons free. We would come back for the rest of the animals later.

My wife sat in the first tub. Franz, who was almost eight years old, sat next to her. Fifteen-year-old Fritz rode behind them. The cargo was in the middle. Then came Jack, eleven, and our second son, Ernest, age thirteen. I stood in the stern.

We cast off and glided into the open sea. We had left the two dogs, Turk and Juno, on board. But when they saw us leave, they jumped overboard and swam behind us.

Soon we could see rocky cliffs and palm trees. The geese and ducks swam toward a small bay. I steered after them.

When we landed, we fell to our knees and gave thanks for our escape. We had no idea what we would find on this island. But we were all alive and on dry land, and for now that was enough.

I selected a large rock to set up camp on. We made a tent from a sailcloth. That night, we drank soup we'd brought from the wreck, using oyster shells as spoons. It was our first meal on our new island home.

Our rooster woke me at daybreak. After morning prayers, Fritz and I went to explore. We searched for signs of sailors from our ship, but found none.

Our hearts were lifted, though, by the peaceful beauty of our new home. A smooth stream flowed from the sea through rocky cliffs on either side. Beyond the cliffs were green grass and tall palms.

We followed the stream past a waterfall and continued on through a grove of calabash trees. We collected several gourds from the trees. The gourds could be carved out to make bowls, spoons, and bottles.

We pushed forward and climbed a rocky summit. We could see far and wide. And we saw that there was no trace of other survivors from the wreck. We were completely alone. A feeling of utter sadness washed over us.

"Cheer up, son," I said after a moment. "Let us remember how lucky we really are."

Fritz agreed and we decided that we would make the best of our situation. On the way down, I cut a reed to use as a weapon if need be. We hadn't gone far when I noticed juice dripping out of it. I tasted it and found it very sweet. It was sugarcane!

We passed the sugarcane and reached a cluster of palms. A group of monkeys chattered from the treetops. Fritz raised his gun. "No!" I cried. "Never take the life of any animal needlessly. A live monkey is of more use than a dozen dead ones. Watch."

I gathered a handful of small stones and threw them at the monkeys. A monkey's instinct is to copy. So they grabbed all the coconuts they could reach from the treetops and threw them right at us!

We picked some up and pierced holes in them. We drank the milk through the holes. Then I split them open and we ate the cream that lined their shells. After this delicious meal, we took a couple of the nuts and started home. Things were beginning to look up.

Suddenly Turk darted after one of the

monkeys. We found a tiny baby monkey hiding in the grass, trembling. When he saw us, he jumped on Fritz's shoulder and held tight to his hair.

"What a jolly little fellow!" exclaimed Fritz. "Do let me try to care for it."

I agreed. Fritz called Turk and seated the monkey on the dog's back. The monkey rode along perfectly at ease.

At the end of the day, we neared the camp and our dear ones came running to greet us. A tempting meal awaited. Several fish and a bird were roasting over the fire. The gravy dripped into a large shell placed beneath them.

We sat down to dinner and used our gourds for the first time. We ate coconuts for dessert. And Fritz fed coconut milk to the little monkey, whom we named Mr. Knips. With my family around me and my stomach full, I began to feel content in our new home.

The next day, I decided to return to the

wreck with Fritz to rescue the animals left there. I also wanted to bring back many of the items on board.

The ship had carried supplies for a new colony. So it had everything we might need. To my great joy, we found guns and knives, kitchen utensils, wine, meat, seeds, nails, matches, and more tools.

We spent the night on board the wreck. In the morning, we made swimming belts for the animals. I caught a sheep. Then I tied a piece of cloth around its belly and hooked some empty tins to it. This done, Fritz and I flung the animal overboard. Our plan worked, and the sheep bobbed in the water! We did the same for all the animals. Each animal had a cord around its neck. We held on to the other ends and rowed for shore, drawing the herd after us.

The sea was calm and my spirits were high. With the supplies and the animals, we could live comfortably for as long as we might be on the island.

Suddenly Fritz yelled and drew his gun. A huge shark was swimming straight for one of our sheep! Fritz fired. The bullet found its mark and the shark sank into the water. The lucky sheep escaped what would surely have been a grisly end.

"Well done, Fritz!" I cried, and steered us safely home.

2

The Tree House

We were greeted on land with shouts of joy. My wife told us that she and the boys had found a beautiful grove of giant trees. The trunks were lifted high off the ground by great arching roots. The leafy branches offered cool shade. And the ground itself was carpeted in soft green leaves.

"If we could build a house in one of those trees, I should feel perfectly happy," she said.

I considered her plan. "Suppose we build your nest in the trees," I suggested, "but keep this rocky place as a fortress."

Everyone was excited about living in the treetops. Before we left, we built a bridge across a nearby stream to make our journey easier.

We packed our bags and placed the bundles on the cow's back. The donkey was also put to work carrying bundles and bags.

We crossed the bridge and were making good progress when the dogs suddenly dashed off. We heard a furious barking, followed by a howling. I had no doubt a dangerous animal had attacked them!

"Father! Come quickly!" cried Jack. "A huge porcupine!"

Sure enough, the dogs had tried to seize the creature and had been wounded by its quills. They would learn to stay away from porcupines in the future!

We marched on until we reached our new home. The site was just as my wife had described.

We unloaded the animals. Then we sat down to rest among the soft leaves on the ground.

Ernest studied the tree closest to us. "What sort of tree is this?" he asked.

"I think these must be wild figs," I replied. Their sweet fruit would be as welcome as their shade.

After a good dinner, we slung hammocks from the arched roots of the tree. We covered the arches with the sailcloth to form a tent.

Fritz, Ernest, and I went to the beach to gather wood and bamboo. Then we set to work on a rope ladder to reach what would become our tree house—thirty feet above the ground.

When the ladder was finished, Jack climbed up, quick as a monkey. "What a grand home we will have here!" he exclaimed. Fritz was soon by his side. I followed with an ax and took a survey of the tree. It was perfect! The branches were strong and close. We could simply lay some planks across them to make floors. We worked until after dark, and rose early the next morning to set to work again.

Fritz and I climbed the ladder. We chopped off the extra branches from the tree so they wouldn't be in our way. We left a few branches to hang the hammocks on and some higher ones to support the sailcloth roof.

My wife tied the wood we had brought to

a rope, and Fritz and I hauled it up. We laid it down on the bottom branches to form a smooth, solid floor. Around this platform we built a wall of planks. Then we threw the sailcloth over the higher branches for a roof. We drew it down and firmly nailed it in place.

Our house was enclosed on three sides by the walls and the great trunk. We left the front open to let in the sea breeze. We then hauled up our hammocks and hung them. It wasn't dark yet, so we cleared the floor of leaves and twigs. We used the rest of the wood to build a table and a few benches.

After working so hard, we flung ourselves on the grass below. My wife set supper out on the table we had made. "Come and taste flamingo stew," she said.

That night, we lit our watch fires and left

the dogs on guard. Then we climbed the ladder. I went last, with Franz on my back. I pulled the ladder up behind us. I felt safer than I had since we landed.

3

ISLAND LIFE

"What shall we do today?" the children asked the next morning.

"On the seventh day, thou shall rest," I replied.

"Is it really Sunday?" asked Jack. "But what shall we do? We can't go to church here."

"The leafy shade of this tree is more beautiful than any church," I said. "We will worship here."

After our simple service, I let the children spend the day as they wished. Jack and I made a little bow and some arrows for Franz to shoot with.

Suddenly we heard a shot over our heads. Two small birds fell at our feet. We looked up and saw Ernest in the branches.

He slipped down the ladder and brought the birds to me. The birds had come to eat the figs from our tree. Since the figs were just now becoming ripe, there would probably soon be large flocks of birds in our trees.

The tropics are known to have a rainy season every year. I had been worried about how we would find food when the rains came. I knew that if we could catch the birds, we could store them for later.

I was still thinking on this when we were called to dinner. During the meal, I suggested we name the different spots on the island. "Let us begin by naming the bay in which we landed."

"I think," said my wife, "that, as thanks for our escape, we shall call it Safety Bay."

This idea was met with approval. We then named our first campsite Tentholm. The islet in the bay we called Shark Island. Our tree house Falconhurst. The first hill we climbed Prospect Hill. The stream by our landing place Jackal River, because we'd seen jackals there. And the rocky heights from which we saw we were alone Cape Disappointment.

The next day, we took a hike to Tentholm. The boys roamed ahead. Presently, we heard a joyful shout. Ernest raced toward me, holding a plant. "Potatoes!" he gasped with sparkling eyes.

"Yes," cried Jack. "Acres and acres!"

"With potatoes, we shall never starve," said I. My heart was easier about the rainy season now. We hurried to the spot. We were so excited that we did not stop digging until every bag, pouch, and pocket was filled.

At Tentholm we collected some of the supplies we had left there. Then we returned home. And after a hardy supper of potatoes and milk, we climbed our tree for the night.

The next morning, Fritz and I took the tub boat to the wreck. Once we were there, we made a raft out of water casks to carry back items too large for the tub boat.

We spent the night on board the wreck. When the sun rose, we carried off everything from our own cabins. We claimed the furniture and window and door frames from the captain's room. We took the officers' chests. One was filled with gold and silver watches, rings, and other jewelry.

I was delighted to discover a number of carefully packed young fruit trees. We also found more tools, sacks of oats and peas, and a harpoon. We loaded the boat and the raft and pushed off.

On our way back to shore, Fritz saw a turtle floating in the distance. I steered closer to have a better look. Suddenly I felt a shock. The boat was being pulled through the water!

To my amazement, I saw that Fritz had struck the turtle with the harpoon. A rope was tied to it, and the creature was running away with us!

"Fritz, what have you done?" cried I. "You will sink us!"

"Oh, Father, I have him!" Fritz shouted with excitement. "Do let us catch this turtle if we can!"

The turtle pulled us to the beach. It was very tired. And no wonder. It had been dragging two heavy boats at full speed! I leapt into the water and pulled out my ax to kill it.

The family soon appeared in the distance with a cart that Ernest and I had made some days before. It required all of our effort to hoist the heavy turtle on board. We added the fruit trees and headed home.

When we got there, I turned the turtle on its back. I cut some meat for our supper.

"What a handsome shell!" cried Fritz. "I should like to make a water trough of that, to stand near the brook and be kept full of clear water."

"That is a capital idea!" I replied.

Ernest then showed me some roots he had found that day in the woods.

My heart leapt with joy. The boy had made a brilliant discovery! "I believe these to be manioc root," I exclaimed. "Cakes called cassava bread are made from it. With these, we will always have plenty to eat!"

The boys and I set to work. Each took a tobacco grater we had taken from the wrecked ship and began grating a manioc root. No one was tempted to taste the flour it made—it looked like wet sawdust!

The next step was to press it to take out the sap. We put the damp powder into bags my wife had made. We laid the sacks on smooth planks. We placed another plank on top of them. We weighted this with everything heavy we could find. The sap flowed to the ground.

I took out handfuls of dry flour and mixed it with water and salt. I kneaded it, forming a cake. I laid it on an iron plate over the fire. Presently, it turned golden brown. I wanted to be certain it was safe, so I gave the cake to two hens and the monkey to eat.

In the morning, we were all very happy to see the hens and monkey in good health.

No time was lost. We began baking bread. Soon we had a pile of tempting cakes. We breakfasted royally.

My thoughts turned back to the wreck. I took Fritz, Ernest, and Jack back to collect more items. Fritz made a wonderful discovery. He found a light sailing ship, called a pinnace. It was carefully packed away in pieces.

I was determined to possess the pinnace! We loaded the boat and the raft with butter and flour and other items. Then we studied the pinnace. The problem was, it was stowed in a very narrow space. We had no room to put the parts together there. But the parts were too heavy to move.

Our days were now spent on the wreck. We went to work with axes, breaking down the compartment to clear space. First we cleared an open area around the pinnace. Then we put the parts together.

At length, the pinnace was ready to be launched. But it was imprisoned within the wreck!

I was almost in despair when I had an idea. I found a large cannon and filled it with gunpowder. I placed it so that when it exploded, it would blow out the side of the wreck.

I told the boys to get in the boat. Then I

lit the match and hurried after them. We were already ashore when it came. A flash! A roar! A burst of smoke!

We sprang back into the boat and rowed for the wreck. When we rounded the far side, a marvelous sight awaited us. The compartment where the pinnace rested was torn open.

"Hurrah!" I shouted. "She is ours!"

The boys followed me into the opening. I placed rollers beneath the pinnace. And with some effort, she slipped into the water.

We were ready to surprise my wife. We spread the sail, and the pinnace glided

swiftly through the water. When we entered the bay, the boys fired a salute.

"What a charming boat!" exclaimed my wife.

I saw all this hard work was making the boys very strong. But it was having another effect upon their clothes. I decided to visit the wreck one last time to see if we could find new clothes.

The three older boys and I found the wreck as we had last seen her. We rummaged through all that was left on her. Sailors' chests, cloth, tables, benches, window shutters. We made several trips back and forth, and soon everything was ashore.

Before we left, I lit a fuse to blow up the brave ship that had carried us from Switzerland. It saddened me to do so, but I knew that even her battered decks could be put to use. Darkness came. A pillar of fire rose from the water. A roar boomed across the sea. And we knew our old ship was no more.

The next day, we were cheered to see the shore lined with planks and beams from the wreck. The ship had been good to us to her very end.

4

FALCONHURST

The peaceful shade of our tree seemed more delightful than ever after the hard work of the past few weeks.

Around this time, I came up with a new weapon for my boys. "This is a lasso," I said. "One end is swung around and around, and then thrown toward the animal you wish to catch."

But even better than the lasso was another discovery. One afternoon, I noticed some bushes loaded with white berries. We could use these berries to make wax candles. We filled a canvas bag with them.

The next morning, the boys woke with the word "candle" on their lips.

We were soon at work. We threw the berries into an iron pot on the fire. The wax melted and rose to the top of the berry juice. My wife prepared wicks and we dipped them into the wax. We repeated this until they became thick, sturdy candles. For the first time Falconhurst was brilliantly lit!

Next we planted the fruit trees in two lines from Falconhurst to Family Bridge. Between them, we laid down a road.

We were eating supper when our donkey, Grizzle, suddenly let out a loud bray and ran away. We chased him. But we could not catch up.

In the morning, Jack and I took the dogs to search for him. After a while, we saw his tracks mixed with other tracks. In the distance, I could see animals grazing. We suddenly found ourselves face to face with a herd of buffalo!

Before I could stop them, one of the dogs rushed forward and seized a buffalo calf. The herd went on the attack! They were upon us in no time! I drew a pistol and fired. The herd stopped and galloped off.

Clever Jack unwound his lasso and cast it toward the calf. It drew tight around his hind legs. We fastened it to a stout bamboo.

The young buffalo followed us quietly and, after a time, allowed us to lay a bundle on his back.

On the way home, the dogs peered into a cleft in the rocks. A jackal jumped out and

attacked them! The jackal was no match for the dogs. But from the way she fought, I knew her young must be near. Jack crept into the cave and emerged with a beautiful yellow pup. He named the pup Fangs.

Back at home, the buffalo and the jackal pup delighted the others. Then they surprised me with a new animal of their own. While we were gone, Fritz had found a young eagle. I suggested he train it to hunt.

Soon after this, my wife came to me with an idea. "I wish," she said, "that you would build a staircase to our tree house."

I thought it over. I had often thought our great trunk might be hollow. If that were true, we could build a staircase inside it.

We got to work. First we cut a door in the base of the tree. We fitted into it the door we had brought from the captain's cabin. We then began building a spiral staircase. We used a sapling as the center and planks from the wreck for the steps. Up and up, we built. We cut windows in the trunk as we went to give us light and air.

Meanwhile, our animals were doing well. Juno and Turk had a fine litter of puppies. Ernest and Jack made a basket for Mr. Knips. They strapped it to the monkey's back. Then they taught the little fellow to climb trees and bring the fruit down in the basket.

One morning, we were awoken by a terrific noise. Jack thought it was a lion. I agreed with Ernest that it might be a hyena. Fritz climbed down to see and burst out laughing. *Hee-haw, hee-haw!* It was our donkey, Grizzle, returned to us!

The rainy season was near. So we next

set about building a shelter for our chickens. We made a bamboo roof over the arched roots of our tree.

Every day we loaded our cart and brought in food for the winter. Potatoes, coconuts, sugarcanes, manioc.

When the rains came, we took our furniture and moved downstairs under the roots. The animals and all our supplies were packed in with us. It was so crowded we barely had space to move. During the day, we let the animals out to make more room. At night, Fritz and I would go into the pouring rain to bring them home. Each time we returned soaked to the skin.

We soon became used to the smell of the animals and the smoke from the fire—we had no choice. But time went slowly. The boys played with their pets. Our cow had

had a calf. "Will you look after this little fellow?" I asked Franz.

"Oh yes, Father!" he agreed happily. "I shall call him Grumble. Hear the grumbling noise he makes!"

Ernest sketched, my wife sewed, and Fritz and Jack taught Franz to read. I wrote a journal of all that had happened to us on the island so far. Weeks and weeks went by. We were prisoners while the rain battered down.

5
THANKSGIVING

At length, the winds calmed and the rain finally stopped. Spring had arrived.

No one could have felt more joy than we did as we stepped outside.

Our first task was restoring our nest. It was filled with leaves and torn by the wind.

Fritz and I visited Tentholm. The damage to Falconhurst was nothing compared to poor Tentholm. The tent was ripped to rags, and the supplies were soaked. We'd have to make better winter quarters before the next rainy season.

Fritz suggested that we should hollow out a cave in the rock. It would be hard work, but I decided to try. We began hammering on the rock. For days we kept at it. We made little progress. But on the tenth day, Jack shouted, "Father, my bar has gone right through!" The boy had found a great cavern!

With a shout of joy, we banged on the rock. Pieces fell until the hole was big enough for us to enter.

Jack ran home to tell the others. They all came back in the cart. Jack had also brought all the candles he could find. Silently we marched into a cave of glittering crystal. Crystal pillars rose from the floor like trees and dripped from the ceiling.

I tasted a piece. It was rock salt. Here was an unlimited supply of pure salt!

We turned all our attention to the new house, which we called Rockburg. We decided we would use it for the rainy season and keep Falconhurst for the summers. We cut a row of windows in the rock. We fitted them with the window frames from the officers' cabins. We divided the cave into rooms and built a fireplace and a chimney.

For two months we worked on our salt cave to make it comfortable. We leveled the floors. We made carpet out of wool and hair from the sheep and goats.

It was around this time that we saw something strange in the water. The sea moved as if it were boiling! Hundreds of birds hovered over it.

"A herring bank," I said. "A huge number of herring that come to shallow water to escape larger fish."

We quickly began a fishery. Jack and Fritz stood in the water with baskets. They scooped out the fish. We cleaned them. Then we packed them in salt to preserve them. We would eat well during the next rainy season!

One morning soon after this, I realized that the very next day would be the anniversary of our escape from the wreck. I decided that it should be a day of thanksgiving.

On the anniversary, we talked of everything that had taken place since the storm. I read from my journal and we thanked God for saving us.

Afterward, I announced a "Grand Display of Athletic Sports." My wife and I would be the judges.

"What a wonderful idea! Will there be prizes?" asked the boys.

"Certainly!" I said. "Trumpeters! Sound the openings!"

I waved my arms wildly toward the shady spot where the ducks and geese rested. Up they started, cackling and trumpeting as I had hoped.

We began with shooting. I brought out a board shaped like a kangaroo. The boys fired. Fritz hit the kangaroo's head every time.

Archery followed. I saw with pleasure that the boys were really skillful.

After a break, I started a running match. Fritz, Ernest, and Jack had to run to Falconhurst. The first one to reach the tree had to bring me a penknife I had left there. I gave the signal, and they were off!

Fritz and Jack burst forward with all their effort. Ernest started behind with a good, steady pace. Ernest was smart. I guessed he'd be able to keep up that pace better than his brothers.

Long before we expected them back, we heard galloping. We looked in surprise toward the bridge and saw Jack thundering toward us on Storm, the buffalo.

He waved at us. "I very soon saw that I

hadn't a chance," he explained, "so I came back on Storm so I could see the winner come puffing in."

By and by, the other boys made it back. Ernest held up the knife to show he had won.

Next we tested the young athletes' climbing skills. Jack won easily. He was as lively as a monkey. Riding followed. Each boy rode a different beast. I thought riding was over when little Franz appeared. He was leading Grumble.

"Prepare to see something wonderful!" he said.

Then, taking a whip, he made the animal walk, trot, and gallop on command.

The sports finished with swimming matches.

By this time, it was getting late. We returned home for the prize ceremony. For

shooting and swimming, Fritz won a beautiful hunting knife and a rifle. For running, Ernest won a gold watch. For climbing and riding, Jack won a pair of silver spurs and a riding whip. And for bull training, Franz received a pair of stirrups and a driving whip.

6

TROUBLE
VISITS US

*S*oon after that day, I remembered it was around this time last year when huge flocks of birds came to eat the figs at Falconhurst. We hurried to the nest, where we found the birds already busy with the fruit. I made a sticky mixture of oil and a rubbery tree gum to catch them.

The boys brought rods. I smeared the rods with the mixture. Then we placed them in the treetops.

When the birds landed, they stuck fast. The more they fluttered, the more stuck they became. Eventually they fell to the ground.

The following day was spent in plucking, boiling, roasting, and stewing.

For some time nothing more exciting happened. Then one day Jack came home covered in mud and green slime. He looked like he was going to cry!

"My dear boy, what has happened?"

"I was in the swamp, Father," he said. "I was on a firm spot when I slipped!"

The poor child took a deep breath and continued. "I sunk deeper and deeper. I was soon stuck above my knees! I screamed and screamed. But nobody came!"

At that, Jack knelt and patted Fangs fondly. "At last, who should appear but my faithful jackal, Fangs. I cut down all the swamp reeds I could reach. Then I leaned on them and kicked until I got my legs free. Fangs ran back and forth, barking. Finally, I caught hold of his tail and he dragged me to firm ground."

"A fortunate escape, my boy!" I cried. "Fangs is a hero!"

With Jack safe once more, we returned to our work. Now that the cave was almost finished, we built an aqueduct to supply it with freshwater. We made it with pipes of hollow bamboo. My wife said she was as pleased as if we had made her a marble fountain.

The rainy season was again near. So we collected stores of roots, fruits, grains, potatoes, rice, guavas, acorns, and pine cones.

Heavy clouds gathered. We moved the animals and ourselves to the salt cave.

We still had much to do to make the cave even more comfortable. With Jack's help, I made a chandelier out of a ship's lantern to light the cave.

Ernest and Franz made shelves for a library. They placed on them the books we'd saved from the wreck.

We built tables and benches. I added a wide porch along the front of the cave.

We amused ourselves by opening chests from the ship we hadn't looked into yet. We found all sorts of treasures—mirrors, a musical box, elegant writing tables, and clocks. Our cave soon looked like a palace!

Finally, the thunder quieted and the rainy season ended. I was seated with my wife and Fritz beneath the shade of the veranda one day when Fritz jumped up.

"I see something strange in the distance,

Father! It's coming toward the bridge!"

My wife and the boys retreated into the cave. They closed up all the entrances, then kept watch, with guns at the windows.

Fritz and I stayed outside, looking at the creature through my spyglass.

"It is a giant serpent!" I cried at last.

The monster reptile advanced with writhing movements. From time to time, it reared its head to the great height of fifteen or twenty feet!

As it crossed the bridge, we withdrew into the cave. We barricaded everything at the door and waited with beating hearts. When the serpent reached the front of the cave, the boys and my wife began firing. These shots startled the monster. He turned and disappeared into the reedy marsh.

I asked that no one leave the cave while the serpent was nearby. And in truth, no one had any desire to do so.

For three days we were kept in suspense and fear. By the third day, we were running out of hay for the animals. I decided to send Fritz with them across the river to find food. We were getting ready to do this when old Grizzle, the donkey, broke free. He galloped straight for the marsh! With horror, we saw the serpent rear up from its lair. Its deadly jaws opened wide. Grizzle was doomed.

Swift and straight, the serpent was upon him. He wound round him, then swallowed the poor donkey whole. When the serpent was finished, he lay quiet. Now was the moment for attack!

The boys and I crept forward with our guns. We fired together. A quiver ran through the mighty frame. And the serpent lay dead.

7

BEARS AND OSTRICHES

We had faced our greatest danger yet. But I was worried that another serpent might appear.

I suggested a trip to search the area where the serpent had come from. The whole family decided to join me.

We packed the tent and our supplies in the cart. We harnessed it to Storm and Grumble and started off.

After a time, we reached a place near the

sugarcanes where we had once built an arbor. We spread the sailcloth over it to make a tent.

The three older boys and I, and all the dogs except Juno, set off to explore. My brave wife remained in camp with Franz. As we went, we found that the shrubs had been broken down. The serpent had clearly been through.

We decided to build strong defenses there to stop future invaders. Then we continued on. We crossed a stream and soon found ourselves in a desert. We stopped to eat beneath the shade of an overhanging rock.

While we were eating, Fritz cast his eyes over the plain before us.

"Is it possible that I see horsemen?" he said.

We passed the spyglass around. Jack and

Ernest agreed that they looked like men on horseback. But when I looked, I saw that they were very large ostriches.

"They would be difficult to catch," I said. "Ostriches are very fast."

We thought no more about the ostriches and made our way to a shady valley. Ernest and one of the dogs were ahead. Suddenly we heard a cry of terror.

We rushed forward.

Ernest met us. "A bear, Father!" he shouted. "He is coming after me!"

To my alarm, *two* huge bears appeared!

Fritz and I both fired. The bullets hit the monsters, but merely wounded them. The bears roared in rage! The dogs rushed at them. We dared not fire in case we hit one of the hounds. Instead, we advanced with loaded pistols. When we were just a few paces away, we fired. One was shot through the head. The other was rearing back, about to spring on Fritz! The bullet found his heart. They both fell dead.

"Thank Heaven!" I cried.

Jack raised a shout of victory.

"We shall have a couple of splendid bearskin rugs," said Fritz.

It was getting late. So we dragged the huge beasts into their den to wait until we could skin them. Then we headed to camp for the night.

In the morning, we returned to the den

and went to work. We smoked the meat on the spot and stored the fat. We saved the paws to cook later.

I woke the boys at dawn. Fritz, Jack, Franz, and I, with two of the dogs, galloped off. We were going to try to capture one of the ostriches we'd seen earlier.

We soon came to the spot where Fritz had seen them. Jack and Franz rode ahead. They were some distance from us when four ostriches rose from where they were sitting. With a shout, Jack and Franz drove them toward us. Fritz threw his eagle up in the air. The eagle swooped down on the head of one of the birds. The ostrich was so confused that he slowed down. Jack hurled his lasso and snared the giant bird. We looped a cord around his legs so that he could not run off.

"I am going to make a saddle for him and ride him," said Jack.

His brothers wanted the interesting creature for themselves and raised a cry at Jack's plan. "Come, come," I said. "I think that Jack has a right to the ostrich, seeing as he was the one who brought it down."

We headed homeward at dawn. The ostrich trotted between Storm and Grumble. He was livelier than they were, but the two beasts kept him in check.

We were soon once more settled at Rockburg.

We tied the ostrich between two bamboo posts out front. After a month of training, the ostrich would trot, gallop, and obey our commands.

At length, we all learned to ride Master Hurricane. He was so fast we could travel between Rockburg and Falconhurst in almost no time!

In this way, time passed, and another winter arrived, with great black clouds and terrific storms. We gave up our daily trips. The time inside dragged. And our spirits were low.

"Let's make a kayak," suggested Fritz. "Something swifter than what we have, that will skim over the water."

Everyone was delighted with the idea. We built the boat's skeleton of whalebone. We used bamboo to strengthen the sides and to make the deck. We left a little square hole for us to sit in.

By the time the kayak was done, the rain had passed and the sun again shone.

The day came when Fritz was ready to make his trial trip. He boldly ventured into the strong current of Jackal River. From there, he was rapidly carried out to sea! This was more than I had bargained for!

Ernest, Jack, and I gave chase in our boat. After some time, we soon heard Fritz's cheery halloo. The kayak darted from behind a point of land. "Come to this beach," cried Fritz. "I have something to show you!"

With amazement, we saw a young walrus. It had been killed by a harpoon.

"I congratulate you, my boy! But you should not have gone out of the bay."

"I was carried along by the current," said Fritz. "I could not help myself. Then I saw a herd of walruses. I chased them and harpooned this fellow. I should like to fasten the head, with these grand white tusks, on the kayak. I will call it the Sea Horse."

"We must certainly carry away the ivory tusks," I agreed. "But hurry, a storm is brewing."

We cut off the head of the walrus and sliced strips of its skin. Fritz was soon skimming over the water on his kayak with its fierce figurehead. We followed at a slower rate.

Meanwhile, black clouds had gathered. A tremendous storm came on. Fritz was out of sight.

Ernest, Jack, and I lashed ourselves to the boat so that we would not be washed overboard.

Wind whipped the ocean. Rain fell. Lightning flashed. The storm picked up. Then the sky began to clear as suddenly as it had darkened. I had never lost hope for us. All my fears were for Fritz—alone in his little boat. At last, we entered Safety Bay.

To our surprise and delight, we saw Fritz with his mother. We gave thanks for our spared lives.

8

AFTER TEN YEARS

"We spend our years as a tale that is told," said King David.

I thought of these words as I reviewed ten years in my journal.

Time was passing away.

Our sons were growing up.

Over the years, we had discovered many interesting animals lived on the island with us—gorillas, elephants, and even kangaroos. Rockburg and Falconhurst remained our winter and summer homes. We had made many improvements. There were fountains, trellised verandas, and plantations around Rockburg. We had cleared and drained the swamp. It was now a large lake. Stately black swans and snow-white geese sailed on its waters. We had also built a watchtower on Shark Island.

We had all enjoyed good health in these ten years. The boys grew into fine, handsome fellows. But my wife and I were nearing old age. And I worried about my sons' futures. What kind of life would they have on the island with no chance for families of their own?

The boys began to feel restless. They often went on trips to explore. One such time, Fritz had been off for a full day in his kayak. "Welcome back, Fritz!" I cried when he returned. We all gathered around him.

"My trip has led to interesting discoveries," he told us. "I left the harbor this morning. I wanted to explore farther than we have along the coast. After an hour and a half, I saw a magnificent archway in the side of a cliff. I passed through it into a huge cavern." His eyes sparkled with excitement.

"The water beneath me was crystal clear," he went on. "I could see beds of shellfish in it. I hooked up several clusters. I landed on the beach and flung them on the sand. Then I went to fetch more. I supposed the sun didn't agree with them. For when I came back, they were all wide open. I looked at them and found these pearly balls." He held out his hands.

"You have discovered treasure!" I exclaimed. "Why, these are pearls! They will

be a source of wealth should we ever again be in the civilized world."

Later, Fritz drew me aside. He had not told us everything about his trip. While leaving Pearl Bay, he had been attacked by seabirds. He had struck one with the boat hook.

"The bird fell stunned into the water," said Fritz. "I raised it to the deck of the kayak. Then I saw a piece of rag was wound round one of its legs. To my astonishment, English words were written on it! It said, 'Save an unfortunate Englishwoman!'" He showed me the rag.

"My brain whirled," continued Fritz. "Can it be that we are not alone? I tore a strip from my handkerchief. On it, I wrote, 'Do not despair! Help is near!' I bound it to the bird's leg. The bird slowly revived and took flight. Oh, Father, shall I be able to find this woman?"

I listened to Fritz's story with growing surprise. I could hardly believe it! "You were wise not to excite the others," I said. "The words may have been written long ago. The unhappy stranger may have since perished."

We decided that Fritz should go in search of the lady.

The boys were busily opening the oysters. All thoughts turned to a trip to Pearl Bay to build a pearl fishery. No one noticed that Fritz had a more important voyage in view.

We boarded the pinnace. Fritz set off on his kayak. After a time, we followed him through the archway that led to Pearl Bay.

We found a landing place by a sparkling stream. We anchored and set up camp onshore. After two days of work, we had a giant pile of shells on the beach. Late in the evening on the last day, we stopped work. We ate dinner and went to bed.

In the morning, we followed Fritz out of the bay under the archway. Then, waving his hand to me, Fritz turned in the opposite direction.

I told his brothers that he was exploring more of the coast. I did not tell them he was looking for a lady.

9

The Stranger

My wife and Franz were happy to see us return safely. But Fritz's absence startled them. Five days passed. Fritz remained gone. I could not hide my worry. I decided to search for him.

The whole family sailed in the pinnace on a bright morning. The sunshine and sea breeze put us all in high spirits.

"Look!" cried Franz after some time. He pointed to a spot on the water.

It was Fritz's kayak! Ernest took the trumpet. "Fritz ahoy!" he shouted.

In a moment, the brave boy was on board. We kissed his face heartily.

Fritz cast me a glance full of meaning. "I can lead you to an island where you can anchor," he said. "It contains all sorts of wonderful things."

He sprang back into his kayak. He piloted us to a little island in the bay. There was no doubt now as to Fritz's success. To prepare my wife for the surprise, I told her about the message. She was almost over-come with excitement.

"Why did you wait with such happy news?" she asked.

"I didn't want to raise your hopes in case Fritz found nothing," I replied.

The boys jumped ashore as soon as the

anchor was dropped. We followed Fritz through a thicket. On the other side, we saw a hut. A cheerful fire burned at the entrance. The boys looked at each other in confusion.

Fritz dived into this shelter. When he came out, his face shone with joy. To our amazement, he was leading a young lady by the hand. The boys stared in disbelief.

"Hello," said the girl shyly.

"Will you not welcome her to our family?" asked Fritz.

We were all speechless—in all our years on the island, we had never dared hope to meet another soul! Where had she come from? How had she survived on these shores? I regained my voice first. "We will indeed!" I exclaimed. I held out my hands to the fair stranger. My wife, too, embraced the girl. The boys were elated.

They were full of questions and nearly dancing from excitement. When they had recovered a bit from the shock, they ran down to the boat to get supplies and set up camp. This done, my wife set out a meal. The boys were eager to make their guest feel at home and did their best to amuse her. By the time we sat down to supper, she was laughing and chattering with the rest. The girl admired the various dishes and kept up a lively conversation.

After the feast, we cheered and drank to her health. Then she was led to quarters we had readied for her on the pinnace.

Fritz joined his brothers in three cheers for their new sister. When the boys quieted, he told us her story.

"Jenny Montrose is the daughter of a British officer," he explained. "He served in India, where Jenny was born. Her mother died when she was only three. When she was seventeen, her father received orders to return to England with his regiment. Jenny went on board a different ship. A week after Jenny left, a storm arose. It drove the ship off course. Leaks sprung in all directions. The crew took to the boats. After many days, land was first sighted. Jenny's boat capsized while trying to land. Jenny alone reached the shore. She's lived here these past three years."

After Fritz's tale, we sat in silence, letting the story sink in. We knew better than anyone how hard it was to survive on these islands. To think this brave girl had managed for so long entirely on her own! A great yawn from Fritz drew our attention from these thoughts and we retired for the night.

The next morning, we started home. Jack and Fritz went ahead in the kayak. We glided out to sea.

In due time, Shark Island came into sight. "Oh!" cried Jenny. In astonishment, she gazed at our watchtower, with its guardhouse and waving flag. We steered toward Safety Bay. Fritz and Jack greeted us and helped their mother and Jenny ashore. They led the way through the gently sloping gardens and orchards up to Rockburg. Jenny viewed the villa with awe—its shady balcony, its sparkling fountains. "I can scarcely believe we're still far from civilization!" she told us.

I was just as amazed when I saw a table laid out for lunch on the veranda. All our china, silver, and glass were arranged on the tablecloth. There were decanters of wine. Splendid pyramids of pineapples, oranges, guavas, apples, and pears. Platters of venison, fowl, and hams. And a vase of flowers rose in the center. Fritz and Jack had made a perfect welcome feast.

Jenny took the place of honor between my wife and me. When the banquet was over, the boys showed their new sister the wonders of Rockburg. They led her around the house, cave, stables, gardens, fields, and boathouses and begged her to make herself comfortable. "Thank you," she whispered, her eyes filling with tears of joy.

That night, I slept more soundly than I had in some time, knowing that a new daughter was safely under our roof.

10

THE MYSTERIOUS GUNS

Another rainy season passed. In the evenings, Jenny and the boys took turns reading or telling stories in our cozy study. It was truly a happy time. When the rain stopped and the sun again smiled upon us, we could scarcely believe it had gone so fast.

We visited our settlements to set things back in order. It fell to Franz and Jack to clean the guns on Shark Island. Once this was done, they fired them for practice.

No sooner had they done so when, as if in answer, we heard three guns booming across the water.

We stopped, speechless. Had we really heard strange guns? All sorts of feelings washed over us. Joy, hope, doubt. Were we about to be rescued? Or did these sounds come from a pirate who would rob and murder us?

We fired again and waited.

For some minutes there was silence. Then an answering shot sounded in the distance.

Fritz and I at once prepared for a journey. We armed ourselves with our guns and paddled away in the kayak.

For nearly an hour we headed in the direction from where we had heard the guns. We didn't see anything. Then we rounded a cape and all our doubts vanished. Joy filled our hearts! A large ship was anchored in the cove—and she was flying the English colors!

We saw by the camp set up onshore that the ship would remain for several days. We decided to return later, when we could show ourselves in better form.

We went back to Rockburg and told everyone what we had seen. Everyone was in a state of the greatest excitement. The rest of the day was spent getting ready. We scrubbed the decks of the pinnace and polished the guns. My wife repaired our clothes.

At the break of morning, we gathered for breakfast. We ate quickly and in silence. Our hearts were too full to talk.

Fritz and Jack slipped out and gathered

from the garden baskets of fruit to present to the strangers.

We all boarded our pinnace and set sail, with the kayak in tow. To the utter surprise of the strangers, we rounded the cape!

What a strange sight we must have looked! To see a pleasure yacht cruising on this shore that everyone thought was uninhabited.

Fritz and I stepped into the kayak and

rowed toward the ship. In a minute, we were on her deck. The captain welcomed us and asked us who we were.

I told him an outline of our story and of Jenny's.

"Then," said the officer, "let me thank you in the name of Colonel Montrose. For it was the thought of finding the brave girl that led me to these shores. The colonel has never lost hope for his daughter."

One of the officers was sent to the pinnace, and the rest of my family was soon on board.

Our kind host greeted them warmly. At lunch, the captain told us that a sickly gentleman named Mr. Wolston, his wife, and two daughters had sailed with him. They were resting on land.

We were eager to meet the family. In the afternoon, we paid them a visit.

We found Mr. Wolston seated by a tent, enjoying the sea breeze. He and his family were delighted to see us. We stayed with them until it was too late to return home. The captain offered tents to the boys. The rest of us spent the night on the pinnace.

That night, I had a long talk with my

wife about whether we wished to return to Europe. Neither of us knew what the other was thinking. But we discovered that in both our hearts, we wished to adopt New Switzerland as our home.

My dear wife told me she desired nothing more than to spend the rest of her days on the island. She had become fond of the place. However, she would only want to stay if at least two of her sons also wished to live here. If her other two children chose to return to Europe, she hoped that they would try to send new colonists to join us.

I heartily approved of this idea. We agreed to mention it to the captain. The next morning after breakfast, we asked the captain to visit us at Rockburg. We also invited Mr. Wolston and his family.

Fritz and Jack hurried off to prepare.

They were followed by the English ship and our pinnace.

What words can express the amazement of our guests when they rounded the rocky cape and the splendor of Rockburg lay before them?

Still greater was their surprise as an eleven-gun salute boomed from Shark Island, where the English flag floated on the morning breeze. Poor Wolston seemed to revive with the very idea of the peace and beauty of our island home.

The scene at the harbor and all round Rockburg was full of merriment as the company took in its many sights. At length, we all sat down to talk. But the young people were again soon roaming about our lawns and avenues.

11

THREE CHEERS FOR NEW SWITZERLAND!

Toward evening, we gathered for supper. Mr. Wolston joined us. The rest he had enjoyed seemed to have given him new life. He told us he wanted to stay on the island with his wife and their eldest daughter.

I welcomed this idea, saying that my wife and I wished to remain for the rest of our days in New Switzerland.

"Hurrah! New Switzerland forever!" the company shouted. They raised their glasses.

"Long life and happiness to all who make New Switzerland their home!" added Ernest.

To my great surprise, he leaned forward to ring his glass with mine, his mother's, and Mr. Wolston's. "I wish to remain here, Father," he said.

"Won't somebody wish long life for those who go away?" asked Jenny.

"Three cheers for England and Colonel Montrose," cried Fritz. "Success and happiness to us who sail to Europe—I among them!" The roofs rang with cheering.

"Well," I said, "since Fritz is going to

England, he must bring happiness to Jenny's mourning father and return his dear daughter to him. Ernest chooses to stay with me. His mother and I rejoice at this decision. And now what is Jack's choice?"

"I mean to stay here," Jack replied. "When Fritz is gone, I will be best rider in New Switzerland! The fact is," he added with a laugh, "I expect I'd be sent to school if I returned."

"A good school is exactly what I want," said Franz.

"You may go, my dear son," I told him. "And God bless all our plans."

The captain agreed with our decisions. "Three cheers for New Switzerland!" he cried.

Deep emotion stirred every heart. Many of us were beginning a new life. As for myself, a weight rolled from my heart. I thanked God that it had worked out this way.

After this, we prepared for the departure of the dear ones bound for England. Everything was provided and packed up that could add to our children's comfort and help them in England. Large shares of coral, furs, pearls, spices, and other valuables would give them a good position in the world.

To my and my wife's delight, Fritz told me of the attachment between himself and Jenny. My wife and I had suspected it. We loved the girl dearly and gladly gave our consent for their engagement.

On the evening before we parted, I gave Fritz the journal I had written since the shipwreck. I hoped that it might be published.

"Our story shows the benefits of knowledge and of loving families," I said. "It brings me pleasure to think that others might see it."

Night came. For the last time my whole family slept under my care. Tomorrow, this closing chapter of our journey will pass into the hands of my eldest son.

From far away, I greet thee, Europe!

Like thee, may New Switzerland prosper—good, happy, and free!

Johann David Wyss was born in Bern, Switzerland, in 1743 and became a pastor as an adult. When his four sons were little, he told them imaginative stories of a shipwrecked family. His tales were based on the 1719 book by Daniel Defoe, *Robinson Crusoe,* about a man cast away on an island. One of his sons collected Johann Wyss's stories together and edited them, and in 1812, *The Swiss Family Robinson* was published. It became famous almost right away and since then has been translated into many languages.

**If you liked this thrilling adventure,
you won't want to miss . . .**

TREASURE ISLAND

by Robert Louis Stevenson
adapted by Lisa Norby

I scrambled onto the deck. Israel Hands lay nearby, alive but wounded.

"I am taking over the ship," I told him.

Mr. Hands looked up at me. "Very well, Captain Hawkins," he said. "I'll obey you. I have no choice."

For a few minutes I was so busy that I almost forgot that Mr. Hands was just pretending to be badly hurt. But all of a sudden something made me turn around. He had sneaked up behind me! He pulled out the knife. Then he charged.

20,000
LEAGUES UNDER THE SEA

BY JULES VERNE
ADAPTED BY JUDITH CONAWAY

A volcano burned in the distance. Lava poured from the volcano. The red-hot rocks lit up an entire city.

For it was a city I saw there. I could see towers, palaces, houses, stores. All were lying in ruin. Beyond the city I could see what was left of a large wall.

Captain Nemo picked up a soft rock. With it he wrote on a piece of flat black stone:

ATLANTIS

The Adventures of Tom Sawyer

by Mark Twain
adapted by Monica Kulling

The next day Tom and Huck walked back to the haunted house.

Inside was a dirt floor with weeds growing everywhere. The fireplace was crumbling. And cobwebs hung from the ceiling like curtains!

The boys climbed a rickety staircase to look upstairs. They peeked in a closet in the corner. But nothing was in it. As they turned to go back downstairs, Tom heard a noise.

The boys lay on the floor and peered through a knothole. Two men were entering the house!